DRAGON'S
Halloween

Read more DRAGON books!

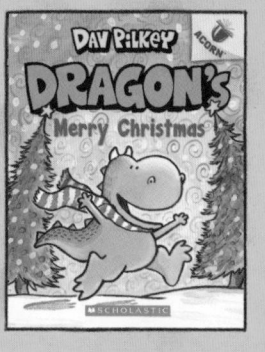

DRAGON'S
Halloween

DAV PILKEY

ACORN™
SCHOLASTIC INC.

For Herb Sandberg

All rights reserved. Published by Scholastic Inc., *Publishers since 1920.* SCHOLASTIC, ACORN, and associated logos are trademarks and/or registered trademarks of Scholastic Inc.

The publisher does not have any control over and does not assume any responsibility for author or third-party websites or their content.

No part of this publication may be reproduced, stored in a retrieval system, or transmitted in any form or by any means, electronic, mechanical, photocopying, recording, or otherwise, without written permission of the publisher. For information regarding permission, write to Scholastic Inc., Attention: Permissions Department, 557 Broadway, New York, NY 10012.

This book is a work of fiction. Names, characters, places, and incidents are either the product of the author's imagination or are used fictitiously, and any resemblance to actual persons, living or dead, business establishments, events, or locales is entirely coincidental.

Library of Congress Cataloging-in-Publication Data

Names: Pilkey, Dav, 1966– author, illustrator.
Title: Dragon's Halloween / Dav Pilkey.
Description: [New edition] | New York : Acorn/Scholastic Inc., 2020. |
Series: Dragon ; 4 | Originally published by Orchard Books in 1993. |
Summary: Dragon is looking forward to Halloween: carving pumpkins, attending a costume party, and making pumpkin treats — but as usual things do not go smoothly.
Identifiers: LCCN 2018040744| ISBN 9781338347494 (hc : alk. paper) |
ISBN 9781338347487 (pb : alk. paper)
Subjects: LCSH: Dragons — Juvenile fiction. | Halloween — Juvenile fiction. |
Humorous stories. | CYAC: Dragons — Fiction. | Halloween — Fiction. |
Humorous stories. | LCGFT: Humorous fiction.
Classification: LCC PZ7.P63123 Dsh 2020 | DDC [E] — dc23
LC record available at https://lccn.loc.gov/2018040744

10 9 8 7 6 5 4 3 2   20 21 22 23 24

Printed in China 62
This edition first printing, July 2020
Book design by Dav Pilkey and Sarah Dvojack

Contents

Six Small Pumpkins

It was October,
and all the world was orange and brown.
Dragon walked through the autumn leaves
in search of a giant pumpkin.

2

"I will find a pumpkin as big as a house," said Dragon.
"Oh, what a scary jack-o'-lantern it will make."

But when Dragon got to the pumpkin patch,
all of the big pumpkins were already gone.
Only six small pumpkins were left,
and they were much too small to be scary.

Dragon loaded the six small
pumpkins into his cart
and brought them home anyway.

Later, as Dragon sat carving
his small pumpkins,
a fox and a crocodile came by.

"What are you doing?" asked the fox.

"I'm making scary jack-o'-lanterns,"
said Dragon.

"Those pumpkins are too small to be scary,"
said the fox.

"Just wait," said Dragon.

Dragon took one of the pumpkins
and poked branches into its sides.

"That pumpkin looks stupid,"
said the crocodile.
"No one will be afraid of your silly
jack-o'-lanterns!"

"Just wait," said Dragon.

Dragon put candles into the pumpkins,
and they all lit up bright and orange.

"Ha, ha, ha, ha, ha!" laughed the fox
and the crocodile.

"We've never seen such funny jack-o'-lanterns
in all our lives!"

"Just wait," said Dragon.

Finally, Dragon stacked the pumpkins
on top of one another
until they were very tall.

The fox and the crocodile
stopped laughing.
Their eyes became wide.
They began to tremble and shake.

The fox and the crocodile ran off
through the woods,
screaming in terror.

"What's the matter with them?"
said Dragon.

Dragon scratched his big head and looked up at the jack-o'-lanterns.

"Aaah! Eeeh! Aaah!" screamed Dragon.

Dragon ran into his house
and hid under the bed.

"I did not know
that six small pumpkins could be so scary!"
said Dragon.

2
The Costume Party

It was Halloween night,
and Dragon was very excited.
He had been invited to a
Halloween costume party.

Dragon tried to think of
a scary costume to wear.

Dragon could not decide whether to be
a witch, a vampire, or a mummy.
He thought and thought,
and scratched his big head.

"One costume would be very scary," said Dragon, "but **three** costumes would be very, **very**, VERY, scary!"

So Dragon decided to wear all three costumes at the same time.

VAMPIRE COSTUME

First, Dragon put on a witch's hat and nose.

"I feel scary already," said Dragon.

Next, Dragon put on a vampire's cape
and teeth.
Dragon could not talk very well
with vampire teeth in his mouth.
"Flmmm flmmm flbm mmm fmm,"
said Dragon.

Finally, Dragon wrapped himself up
just like a mummy.

Dragon hoped his costume would not be
too scary.

Dragon walked through the woods
to the big costume party.

Suddenly, the wind began to blow.

"FLASH!" went the lightning.

"BOOM!" went the thunder.

And DOWN came the rain.

29

When Dragon finally got to the party,
he was soaking wet,
and his costume was ruined.

All of the animals began to laugh.

"Look at Dragon!" they cried.
"Oh, what a silly costume!"

The animals laughed and laughed,
and Dragon felt terrible.
He walked over to a bench in the corner
and sat down next to a big pumpkin.

Suddenly, the bench broke,
and the pumpkin flipped high
into the air.

SPLAT!

Dragon was very dizzy.
He stumbled around the room
covered with slimy orange pumpkin goop.

When the animals saw Dragon,
they screamed in terror.

"Eek! It's a monster!" cried the duck,
who jumped into the pig's arms.

"Oh, dear! Oh, dear!" cried the pig,
who jumped into the hippo's arms.

"Help! Help! Help!" cried the hippo,
who jumped into the hamster's arms.

Finally, Dragon pulled the pumpkin
off his head.

"I am not a monster," said Dragon.
"I am only Dragon."

The animals were very relieved,
and soon everyone felt much better.

Well . . . **almost** everyone.

3
The Deep Dark Woods

The moon was full,
the sky was dark,
and the stomach was empty.

Dragon was **very** hungry.
He walked home through
the spooky forest
thinking of good things to eat.

Softly, the wind began to blow.
Whoo . . . whoooo . . .
WHoooowwWHHhooowHOOO.

That was a scary sound.

The wet leaves beneath Dragon's feet
went **squish, squish, squish, squish!**
That was a scarier sound.

When Dragon got farther into the forest,
he heard the scariest sound of all.

"Grrr . . . grrr . . . GRROWWWL!"

For a moment, everything was silent.
Then suddenly,

"Grrr . . . grrrr . . . GRRROWWWWL!"

"What could that awful noise be?"
cried Dragon.

"Grrrrr . . . grrrrr . . . GRRRROWWWWWL!"

The growling got louder and louder.

"GRRRR . . . GRRRRRRRRR . . .
GRRRRRRROWWWWWWWWWWWL!"

Finally, Dragon jumped in the air.

"Help me!" he screamed.
"It's a **monster**!"

High up in the treetops,
a light flicked on.

"What's going on down there?"
shouted a sleepy-eyed squirrel.

"I hear a monster growling!"
cried Dragon.

"That's no monster," yelled the squirrel.
"That's your **stomach**!"

"Now go home and get something to eat
before you wake up the whole forest!"
cried the angry squirrel.

Dragon held his stomach.
It rumbled and growled.
He felt very silly.

All at once, the forest was dark again.
But now, Dragon was too hungry
to be afraid.
He ran and ran all the way home.

When Dragon got home,
he cooked up a giant Halloween feast.
He made pumpkin pies,
pumpkin soup,
pumpkin bread,
pumpkin pizzas,
and pumpkin ice-cream sundaes.

Then, Dragon ate and ate and ate . . .

. . . until he was as round as a pumpkin.

About the Author

DAV PILKEY is the creator of the bestselling Dog Man and Captain Underpants series. He has written and illustrated many other books for young readers, including the Dumb Bunnies series, *The Hallo-Wiener*, *Dog Breath*, and *The Paperboy*, which is a Caldecott Honor book. Dav lives in the Pacific Northwest with his wife.

YOU CAN DRAW DRAGON!

 Draw a heart shape, but leave the bottom open.

 Add Dragon's eyes, nose, and mouth. Put two horns on top of his head.

 Draw Dragon's back, tail, and tummy. Then add his arm and leg.

Draw spikes down his back and on his tail. Don't forget to add his other arm and leg too!

5 Draw grass and a tower of circles.

6 Add buttons to the three bottom circles. Draw a face on the top three circles. Add two stems for horns.

7 Add arms to the jack-o'-lantern. It is so spooky!

8 Color in your drawing!

WHAT'S YOUR STORY?

Dragon makes a scary costume for the party.
Imagine **you** are going to a costume party.
What costume would you wear?
How would you make it?
Write and draw your story!